Blood in the Studio

Blood in the Studio

Jeffrey LaRocque

RoverMedia, Inc.
2014

Cover illustration: Steve MacAdams – www.qbccle.com
Cover art: Brandon Abate – www.noproblemprinting.com

ISBN: 978-0-9909354-0-7

Printed in the United States of America.

First edition, November 2014.

RoverMedia, Inc.
11777 San Vicente Boulevard, Suite 790
Los Angeles, California 90272

Phone: (216) 202-3600
www.RoverRadio.com

Dedication

I dedicate this book, and my first foray into the literary world, to Rover's Morning Glory: Rover, Duji, Dieter, Dumb, Charlie, and Rob and their zany personalities for giving me the inspiration for the characters in this book.

Contents

Acknowledgements

I would like to thank the staff of iHeartMedia, WMMS-FM, Rover's Morning Glory, The Poon Posse and World Wrestling Entertainment for all the inspiration.

CHAPTER 1

Standing on the side of the Pearl River Bridge, looking down one hundred fifty feet into the deep valley below, Larry Jarocque, who's just a regular guy, is thinking about jumping off.

Let's travel back in time and look at the events that led to this.

Four years ago, he was a nobody…driving a truck for an airline catering company called Jet Chefs, hired in January 2001, nine months before the events of 9/11.

He was laid off after seven years with the company. The reason was the economic downturn of 2008 – the airlines were losing money.

He came home and his girlfriend, Vivien, was cooking dinner.

She turns to Larry and asks, "What's the matter?"

Larry thought for a minute on what to say.

Finally he says, "Honey, I got laid off. I was told the company wasn't making enough money so they laid me off."

Now, Vivien knew if something was wrong, she'd know right away by just reading Larry's face.

Vivien was the basic girl next-door type, raised in a typical Irish family. Her parents came to the United States from Ireland when she was two years old. Vivien is 5'7", 125 pounds, jet-black hair, an hourglass figure that could make any man howl like a wolf, and piercing blue eyes…the kind that could grill a Reuben sandwich twenty feet away.

1

Larry met Vivien in 2002, at a Poison concert she was reviewing. When they met, Vivien was the first to notice Larry out of the corner of her eye. He also made eye contact with her. Both introduced themselves, at the same time gazing into each other's eyes. She spoke first in her lush, sexy Irish accent.

"Hi, my name is Vivien. What's yours"?

"My name is Larry," he answered.

"Oh, that's a sexy name," Vivien responded.

Larry then asked, "What do you do for a living, Vivien?"

"I'm a freelance writer for our town's music and club scene," she replied. "What about you Larry?"

"I do airline catering, it's an interesting job," Larry said.

Vivien knew it was love at first sight because she started lactating. Larry knew that he found the one because his unit stood at attention. It looked like the Washington Monument was protruding from his pants.

Later that night, while sitting on the couch watching television, he began thinking of finding another job to help with expenses.

After seven months of unemployment, early 2009, Larry landed a job working in an auto parts warehouse.

Larry was working in his new job for about a year. One day, nearing the end of his shift, his boss, a big jovial Italian named Mario, asked him, "Hey man, didn't you go to Adlai Stevenson High School?"

Larry said in a bewildered tone of voice, "Um, yes I did." Larry graduated from high school in 2000. The boss was shocked to see him, because he graduated four years before, in 1996, while Larry was a freshman.

In high school, Larry was on the P.A. Club, which is similar to a morning radio show. Soon, Larry's voice became familiar to everyone at school, from the administrators, to guidance counselors, teachers and then students. Everyone said Larry had the voice and personality to be in radio.

Larry didn't think about being in radio at that time. He was thinking about wanting to be welder, unfortunately, that goal was dashed when his father was killed in a factory explosion in December 2001. His Mom died from a severe heart attack four years later. Lucky for him, his parents left him the small, two-bedroom house in their will. He also saved money from small odd jobs he worked.

Late one night, Larry and Vivien were watching television and a commercial flashed on the screen. It was for The Stockton Center for Broadcasting. Vivien saw the wide-eyed look on Larry's face.

She asks, "What are you thinking about?"

"Well, I thought that I'm not getting any younger and I want to try to achieve my career goal, and get into radio. What do I have to lose?" he replied. "It's a matter of trying."

Vivien's ears perked up, and she said, "If that's what you're set on doing I support you."

The next morning, they both went down to the school. They met with the admissions representative; he was the kind of guy that knew if talent was staring him in the face.

Then, after a tour, the admissions representative gave Larry an old commercial script. He asked him to read it as if he was on-air. Larry read the script in very crisp precision as if he had been doing radio for years. The admissions representative's jaw dropped so hard, almost as if it actually would've fallen off his face.

3

He was a retired program director from the local radio station WTRD. He wanted to give back to the industry that he worked in for many years by teaching students the basics of broadcasting, and hoping to discover the next big name in radio.

A couple hours later, Larry and Vivien went home. They started to make arrangements to accommodate both his job and school.

Larry called his boss and with the excitement in his voice and asked, "Guess what?"

"What?" Mario answered.

Larry excitedly said, "I took my first step to get into radio!"

"Oh really?" his boss answered.

Larry went on to tell him about his wanting to get into radio. Mario was unsure about Larry getting into radio, because of the moving from city to city that usually goes with it. But he still supported Larry's decision. They talked for about an hour, about how Mario can accommodate Larry's work schedule, so that it doesn't conflict with his school schedule, and sleep patterns.

About two weeks later, Larry was in broadcasting school. Eight weeks into the course is the time when internships open up for the students.

A woman named Destiny walks in, the kind of girl you could salivate and make you want to just pull down your pants and crank it right there. She had a forehead that was made for target practice.

She said that an internship just opened up on the local radio morning show, then explains what the show's style and content is. Grover's Morning Drive is the show's name.

She writes her e-mail address on the dry erase board. Larry, quicker than the Lone Ranger could pull a gun, jots down the e-mail address.

CHAPTER 2

After having lunch with Vivien, he tells her the exciting news, "I have the best news since sliced toast."

Vivien chimes in, "So, did you get the internship?"

Larry knew he had to be honest.

"I tried getting internships at other radio stations in town, but they're not taking interns. But, I got a lead on one, a woman walked into class today," said Larry.

Vivien looked at him with that look when other women are mentioned.

Larry continues, "She just came in, wrote the show producer's e-mail address on the board and leaves."

"Oh, okay," Vivien replied. She suggested in a serious and concerned tone of voice, "Larry listen to me, I've listened to this show and they have edgy and interesting content."

Vivien was relying on her experience as a freelance writer, she fills Larry in.

"There's one interesting aspect of this show you should know," she explained.

"What's that?" Larry asks.

"The show has a shock jock style, they mix current events with drama," said Vivien.

Later that night, after having a sumptuous Italian dinner, they went upstairs to the bedroom.

7

Larry and Vivien were lying in bed and both excited about Larry's prospects of getting into radio. They began to slowly undress one another. He started feeling on her smooth, silky skin, starting from her shoulders moving slowly south, stopping to feel those beautiful, curvy, voluptuous, and firm, 34D boobs...so big and perky; enough to suffocate someone. Then, he began to rub her nipples, the kind you'd want to drink milk from. He cupped his lips on them. Vivien, at same time, was holding his head and massaging her nether region. Then, she began making those cool moans Larry loves to hear.

She then reached down and grabbed his unit - already standing at attention, lying on the bed, flat on her back, spread eagle. Larry then mounted her, at the same time she caressed his unit, massaging it while guiding it into her docking port. Then, Larry went full pile driver pumping up and down. Then, about five minutes later, he erupts like a volcano with slimy, white lava.

She too hits "the summit" and lets out the loudest top-of-the-mountain scream, her favorite line was, "OH MY GOD THAT WAS AWESOME!" Loud enough, if a window was open it could've been heard all the way down the street.

The next morning, Larry got a call from Destiny. She was on the show and helped gather content to talk about on-air and asked Larry a little about himself, and when he can come in for an interview.

Larry tells her, "I can come in tomorrow at 12 noon."

Destiny thought to herself, *We could work with him. We never had a male intern, interesting guy, though.*

"Okay, no problem, we'll see you tomorrow at noon," Destiny said in her thick, sexy Russian accent, then Destiny hung up the phone.

Her family came the U.S. from Russia before Communism fell.

Larry was anxious and excited that he got the interview, but he knew that in the back of his mind just because you have an interview, you don't necessarily get the gig.

Larry went to work that afternoon and sat down with his boss Mario, and told him the news.

"Guess what?" Larry asked.

"What?" Mario answered.

Larry continued, "I got an interview at the radio station for that internship."

"Really?" Mario asked.

"Yep."

Mario reacted by raising his eyebrow, asking him, "What does your girlfriend think?"

"She's cool with it and encouraging me to pursue my career goals." Larry replied.

When Larry arrived at the radio station for the interview, he was greeted by Destiny, the show's off-air producer.

She is 45 years old, 5'7", 125 pounds, has black, long, shoulder length hair, large piercing dark hazel eyes, and was wearing form fitting jeans, a black turtleneck shirt and 4 inch high heel shoes, to make look taller than she really is.

She walked him into to the conference room to do the interview for the internship. Larry was a little nervous not knowing what Destiny would ask him.

They sat down at the table, she offered him coffee, Larry just said, "Just a little sugar and cream."

Destiny began to explain to him the show's content.

"Okay, Larry our content is a little, I would say is kind of risky, are you okay with that?"

Larry, remembering what Vivien told him, replied, "Yes, I am," confidently.

The next question Destiny asked caught Larry a little off guard. She asked Larry, "Are you okay with talking about your personal life?"

He thinks for a second then responds, "Yes, as long as it doesn't get too personal."

Larry, before he made his decision to get into radio, he didn't talk much about his personal life.

"Look, I'm just a regular guy with a girlfriend. We both work," he told her.

"Okay, that's cool," says Destiny.

She led Larry down the hallway to the show's office to meet the rest of the show's cast. In the office, Destiny and Larry walked in, "Meathead, this is Larry. He's our new intern."

Meathead was his radio name. His real name is Mike Webster and he played football and basketball in high school and college. He was the basic jock/chick magnet type of guy. He loved being stuck on himself, and was very proud of physical conditioning, something he still maintains. Meathead looked up from his computer.

"What's up?" he asks.

"Nothing much," Larry responded.

Meathead looked him up and down.

"Do you work out?" he asked.

"Yes," said Larry.

Larry was also very athletic, himself, having wrestled and played football in high school.

After meeting Meathead, Destiny led Larry down the hall to the phone screening room, which has two positions - one for the phone screener, the other for the guy who does production and sound effects used during the show. Marley was the show's sound engineer, a scrawny, nerdy looking guy, about twenty-nine years old.

"Oh, who's this guy, Destiny?" Marley asked in a sheepish but arrogant tone.

She gave Marley a laser-like stare.

Destiny announced sharply, "This is Larry, our new intern."

First thing Marley thought was, *He's going to take my job.* Marley didn't really trust having interns around.

Then, Larry was introduced to the phone screener. Sherlock was his radio name, his real name is Sean Smith. He earned the name Sherlock because when he screens calls, he uses his investigative intuition to make sure the callers stayed on the topic being talked about.

Larry and Destiny went back to the office and talked about when Larry would start interning on the show.

After a long day, Larry comes home and sits on the sofa. Vivien wasn't home from work yet. Larry just sat there and started to watch television, and started thinking about Destiny. With Vivien on her cycle, they couldn't have sex.

Larry began to take matters into his own hands and pulled his penis out. He started to stroke it up and down in long strokes. The longer he did this, the bigger and longer it grew. At the same time he was breathing heavy, and grunting as if having sex. He hits the summit and thick creamy white lava just oozed out, like the fizz in soda under pressure.

Larry pulls himself together just as Vivien walks into the room and sits down next to him. She hugs him and asks him, "Well honey, how'd it go?"

Larry starts to fill her in on his day.

"It went well. I believe I've got it," Larry said. "Destiny said she'd call me tomorrow and let me know."

Vivien was both excited and concerned about Larry getting into radio.

That Friday afternoon, with Vivien working, Larry gets a phone call. It was Destiny.

"Larry, we would like you to start on Monday. Come to the station around 6 AM."

Larry was so excited, he called Vivien at work.

"Guess what?" he asked her.

"What?" Vivien responded in a suspicious tone of voice.

"I start interning on Monday," he said.

"Oh, okay. We'll talk more over dinner. I have to get back to work, I'm finishing an article about our city's most haunted place, the old abandoned Pearl River steel mill."

"Okay, I won't hold you up, I just wanted to give you a heads-up" Larry said.

Larry hung up with Vivien and called Mario at the auto parts warehouse, Mario picks up the phone.

"Hello," he said.

"It's me, Larry. I'm calling to let you know that I got the internship at the radio station."

Mario then asked, "What do you need from me?"

"I need a slight adjustment to my schedule," Larry replied. "I'll work on the show in the morning, then class in the early afternoon."

"Okay, no problem. When do you start interning on the show?" was Mario's next question.

"Monday," answered Larry.

After spending the weekend with Vivien, Larry was up and getting ready to go to the radio station.

When he arrived, Destiny was there to give him the rundown on the show's structure in terms of the format clock that all radio shows follow. Grover came in, and Destiny introduced Larry to Grover, the show's host.

Grover's real name is Sam Schultz, a tall, lanky, single guy, 35 years old, 5'9", 135 pounds. He's a basic metal head, having grown up with music ingrained in his DNA. His parents work in the music business by running a recording studio back home in Las Vegas where he was born and raised, working with some of the biggest names in music. He's been in radio for 15 years and seeing all the changes in the radio industry.

He walks in and asks, "Who's the new guy?"

"This is Larry Jarocque, he's our new intern," Destiny answers.

Grover replies, "Oh, okay, cool." He turns to Larry and asks, "Are you ready?"

Larry, nervous and excited responds, "Yes, I am."

Grover, relying on his many years in radio, tells Larry, "Listen, all you have to do is stay calm and focused. Remember to project your personality with your voice into the microphone. Listeners love that."

Larry took to heart what Grover said.

At precisely 6:30 AM that Monday morning, with Larry in the studio taking in the atmosphere, Grover's Morning Drive goes on-air using AC/DC's 1979 song, *Highway to Hell*, as the intro.

As the show started, Grover did what he did best, brag about what he did over the weekend.

"Over the weekend, I was at this really nice club, I saw this chick that was so hot if you touched her, you'd burn your hand," Grover said. "She's about 5'10", 136 pounds, ash blonde hair, brown eyes, and 38DD creamers and no boyfriend. So, I say to myself, *You know, I could hit that, but after a few drinks.*

Destiny chimes in and asks, "What's up with that?"

Grover continues, "With a few drinks, girls have a tendency to loosen up when it comes to putting out."

"So what?" Meathead cut in. "I'd love that if a girl would put out on a first date, but it never happens to me. I have to take the chick out a few times just to get into her pants."

It was Meathead's go-to line when it came to his own interaction with women. He knew that women have the ability to read him like a book; they knew what he wanted, and they figured they could get something out of him.

Grover turned to Larry and introduced him to the listeners.

"We have our new intern here with us today. His name is Larry Jarocque, and what's interesting is he's our first male intern. Larry, tell us a little about yourself," Grover said into the microphone.

Larry cleared his throat and spoke confidently as if he was doing radio for years.

"To start, I was born and raised in this area, and I have a beautiful girlfriend, named Vivien," Larry replied.

"When was the first time you nailed her?" Meathead inquired.

Larry was stunned for a few seconds, but he answered.

"On our third date," Larry replied.

All were shocked.

"We both kinda knew we were right for each other," Larry continued.

Meathead couldn't believe what he just heard.

"You're lucky, Larry," says Meathead.

"Why's that?" Larry asked. "You have to remember that men and women are wired differently in their way of thinking."

"Women are women, what's the difference?" Marley butts in.

If there's anyone on the show that couldn't grasp that concept, it was Marley. He too has a girlfriend, that's a little smarter and wiser than him.

Grover knew exactly what Larry was going to say next.

"Wait a second, I know what you are going to say. Girls know what guys want, and girls can make guys work for it, am I right?" asked Grover.

Larry responded in amazement, "Yes, you're right."

Destiny, sitting at her microphone, polishing her scrappy-looking toenails and checking her phone was oblivious to what was going on.

Grover turned to her and asked, "Are ready to do The Dirt Sheet?"

The Dirt Sheet is the show's news segment.

Destiny was a television news anchor before getting into radio, but was fired by the TV station. She got fired because she couldn't pronounce words correctly. Larry thought he could teach her to pronounce words that she struggled with. Her background in doing news on television was also helpful in getting a job in radio.

The segment got its name from a wrestling talk segment, and was also Meathead's idea, because he was the show's wrestling know it all. Larry was no dummy when it came to professional wrestling history either.

Grover than asked Larry, "What area of broadcasting are you in-terested in?"

Larry adjusted the microphone and spoke.

"Getting into radio, and maybe television," Larry said.

Grover, ever curious, asked Larry about Vivien.

"So, Larry, tell me a little about your girlfriend," he said.

"Her name is Vivien, she's 25 years old about 5'6", 125 pounds, with ash blonde, shoulder length hair," replied Larry.

Mcathead, being the show's de facto chick magnet, was only interested in one part of a girl's body.

"What size are her creamers?" he asked.

Larry was shocked a little by that question.

"Why would you ask that Meathead?" Larry asked in a somewhat demanding tone.

"Well, you know, just curious," Meathead answered.

Larry remembered what Vivien advised about what they ask about and telling him to be honest with them. Vivien also reminded Larry that comes with the job.

"She's got 34D creamers, so perky you would want caress them and suffocate yourself with them," Larry replied. "Or they'd make a great pillow."

"What's her nationality?" Sherlock the phone screener asked.

"She's Irish," Larry replied.

Marley chimes in, "Oh, an Irish girl? Can't go wrong with that, my girlfriend is Italian and a little hot headed when she gets pissed off."

Destiny finally got into the conversation after doing two things that really got on Grover's nerves - painting her finger and toe nails, and constantly checking her phone - when she should've been paying attention to the show.

Grover speaks, "Destiny what the hell are you doing!?"

"Well, just kinda doing my nails," she replied, in a sheepish tone.

"Well knock it off, that nail polish you use stinks to high heaven, and stop checking your phone also," Grover continued. "Come on, you have a hot date or something? You know her…always desperate for a date. My lord, she's been in radio for ten years, couldn't you save all that hassle for after the show?!"

Larry could see Grover was really upset just by listening to his voice.

As the show continued on, Larry was an integral part and everyone noticed he was very observant of what was going on, picked up on it quickly. After the show, Larry recorded some new re-joins they would play when a show comes back from a commercial break.

Later that afternoon, Larry and Vivien were walking through the park after lunch, and they were talking about each other's day. Vivien asked why Larry was a more excited than normal.

"I'm doing my first interview on tomorrow's show," Larry said.

Vivien wondered who the person was.

"Well, I get to interview legendary porn star, Samantha Sable," Larry reported.

"Oh, really?" asked Vivien in a real questioning tone.

"She's the top porn star out there and will be in town for one night only. I know how you feel, but she's not the least bit interested in me."

Vivien chimes in, "Okay, listen to me. I told you before that they do crazy stuff on-air right?"

Larry answers back, "Yes, I do."

Vivien, leaning on her experience as a freelance entertainment writer, remembers the one stunt involving Samantha they did on-air.

"What was the stunt you remember?" Larry asked.

"That stunt took place about five years ago. They had an intern motorboat her. She smacked him so hard she broke his jaw," Vivien replied. "Larry, just remember this, I've met her a few years ago, and she is one aggressive, busty looking chick."

Larry took what Vivien told him to heart.

CHAPTER 3

That next day on the show, Grover introduced Samantha into the studio.

"Okay, let's bring in porn star, Samantha Sable."

She came into the studio and sat down on the big red velvet couch reserved for the show's guests.

She saw Larry and asked, "Do I know you from somewhere?"

Larry, in a confident voice says, "My girlfriend, Vivien, says she met you a few years ago, about the time we started dating, and she introduced me to you."

Everyone was shocked when they heard that. Grover just sat back and let Larry do the interview. Larry did it like a pro. They touched on everything about Samantha's life from her childhood, odd jobs, and before getting into adult films.

Then, Larry asked, "I still have one question to ask you."

Samantha replied, "What's that?"

"I know you've been doing adult films a long time, have you ever thought about retiring?"

Her ears perked up and responded, "Yes, I have, and I'm getting up there in age and want to settle down and have a long term relationship."

Meathead chimes in and asks Larry, "Why don't you tell the audience what she looks like?"

Larry goes, "Okay."

Now, Samantha also knew Larry would be good at radio because he was smart and had tact.

Larry went right into it, "For those don't know about Samantha Sable, she's a 50 year old with the body of a 25 year old. She's been doing adult films since she was 20; 6'0", 145 pounds, and 38DD creamers. If I had to guess, she has had more meat than a sausage factory. She has taken more than 10,000 dongs in her career."

When Meathead saw her boobs he started drooling like a pit bull.

Samantha was a little nervous and asked Larry, "What's with him?"

Larry replies, "Don't worry he's like that all time when he sees a hot girl, thinking he's going to get lucky."

"Oh, okay, for a minute I thought he was going to vomit."

After the interview was concluded, Larry had his picture taken with Samantha and she departed.

Marley nor anyone else on the show could believe what they just witnessed, except for Destiny. She was out of the studio doing other things, God only knows what that is.

She came back into the studio and says, "Well how did it go, did Larry do the interview?"

Marley spoke in a stunned tone, "Larry did the interview like a pro. How did you learn to do that?"

"My girlfriend is a freelance reporter and taught me how to interview people and be able to make them comfortable talking to you."

Marley's mind began to wonder. He thought, *How the fuck does this guy do it*? For the rest of the show that day, he wrestled with that question.

CHAPTER 4

Larry continued to work at his auto parts warehouse job, going to school, and enjoying weekends with Vivien.

Mario, his boss, was always proud of Larry for being a good employee and getting into radio.

A couple months later, Larry was on his final week of broadcasting school. Leading up to graduation, came his final assignment. He had to do his audition tape and resume. He had a ton of material to draw off from his internship on the show.

With one week left in his internship, everyone on the show, and at the radio station was saddened to see Larry go. He was on his way to a career in radio.

When Larry started to put together his resume and audition tape, he listened to the audio that was recorded while he was interning on the show. He settled on using the interview he conducted with porn star Samantha Sable and several commercials he pre-recorded during his internship at the station.

During the whole time Larry was interning on the show, Marley was getting increasingly jealous of Larry's natural talent.

He thought to himself, I have to find a way to get rid of this guy. I've been here six years as a sound guy. Then, came up with a crazy idea.

About three months after he graduated from broadcasting school, Larry got a phone call. It was Destiny.

"Larry," she said, "Grover wants to meet with you at the radio station."

"Really?!" exclaimed Larry.

"Come in at 11:00 AM tomorrow," Destiny instructed.

Larry was excited about the prospect of actually working where he interned. He met Grover in the show's office and explained everything.

Afterwards, when he came home, Vivien was in the living room proofreading the latest article she wrote about the latest trends in both music and fashion. Specifically, how music influences fashion choices artists make.

She looks up and sees the wide grin on Larry's face, "So what happened Larry?"

"I got hired by the station."

Vivien's eyes lit up, "That's awesome!" she said excitingly.

"I don't know," Larry's voice turned somber.

Vivien asks, "About what?"

"Well," Larry continued, "Marley, the sound guy, doesn't seem to like the idea of me being hired."

"Why's that?" Vivien asked in a concerned voice.

Larry began to explain, "Well, I think Marley doesn't want me on the show, and what his motives are, I don't know, but I would like to find out."

Meanwhile, back at the station, Marley had just come up with an ingenious idea. He would use his ability as a sound engineer to pull a prank on Larry.

That next day was Larry's first day actually working in radio. Marley had to hide in order to pull off his little prank. Everyone on the show was in on it.

Destiny told him, "You are going to interview comedian, Lucy Bell."

"Okay," Larry said.

He went to a production studio to record the interview.

Actually, what Marley did was get another woman who could duplicate Lucy's twangy southern accent to help pull it off.

Marley thought, This going to be so funny. I can't wait to see the look on his face. I'll show him.

Larry, like any good radio personality, read up on Lucy Bell, to do the interview.

Larry introduced himself, "I'm Larry Jarocque, on the phone with comedian, Lucy Bell. Hello Lucy. How are you?"

The woman on the other end wasn't really Lucy, but someone imitating her to throw Larry off.

She responds as Lucy, "Who the hell are you?"

"My name is Larry Jarocque," Larry repeated.

Her response was, "I didn't expect this, someone new to radio to interview me. I was hoping for somebody that has a better radio voice than you."

Larry was shocked at what he just heard. He started to ask about her upbringing, comedy style, and family, but for every question Larry asked, she kind of danced around it.

"What are you, some kind of retarded idiot? Come on, I didn't think you were that stupid! I don't have time for brainless assholes like you!"

All the sudden, she hung up the phone. Marley and the girl doing Lucy's voice impression were laughing so hard that they couldn't breathe. After the interview was finished, it was edited for time.

When the show came back from commercial break, Grover announces, "Alright, Larry just got done interviewing comedian Lucy Bell. Larry, how did it go?"

Larry had a very disappointed look on his face and spoke.

"She was a very difficult person to interview," he said.

Larry didn't even figure out that Marley and some girl played a prank on him. Marley was so confident he could do it again.

Grover asked Larry what happened, already knowing that Marley played a prank on him.

"Well Larry, what happened?" as if acting like he didn't know what was going on.

"I began to talk to her about her life, career, hobbies, etc. She started getting quite defensive. I thought that she was a pleasant person to talk to."

"Well, it happens to the best of us, even me." Grover said as he tried to console Larry.

CHAPTER 5

After the first few months, Larry didn't get picked on too much, until one day.

One Saturday afternoon, Destiny was doing an appearance at a fabric store called Suzy's Sew Shop. A listener handed her a piece of paper.

Destiny was curious, "What is this?" she asked.

The listener told her, "About twelve years ago, I arrested him for soliciting a prostitute. I'm the cop that posed as the prostitute. Ask him about it and I'll bet he'll deny it. He thinks the record was expunged. It wasn't."

Destiny took the information and gave it to Grover.

As Grover reviewed it he asks, "Do you think it's a good idea to embarrass him? Like, I mean it sounds funny, but I don't think it is," Grover said.

"Yeah, but we need to see if Larry really has the thick skin for radio," Destiny told Grover.

He then relented, "Alright then."

All the while Grover and Destiny were talking, Marley was listening to the conversation.

He whispered, "Now's my chance to dick with him again. I did it once, I can do it again."

He snickered with an evil glee.

On Monday's show, Destiny announced, "I have some explosive information on someone on the show. Does anyone have something they want to fess up?"

Everyone looked around.

Then, Marley chimed in, "Larry, what about you? You seem a little nervous."

Larry knew exactly what Marley was referring to.

He spoke up, "Well, just after high school, before I met Vivien, I got arrested for solicitation of a prostitute."

Grover asks, "What happened? Did you have to go to jail?"

Larry began to explain what occurred that night.

"Then how was your case adjudicated?" Grover asks.

Larry answers, "I went to court and pleaded no contest to the charge, and the judge sent me to an intervention program and STD testing. I successfully completed that, and the STD tests all came back negative, so my whole record was expunged."

Sherlock, who's the phone screener, joins in and asks, "Is it possible that you missed a step in the expungement process?"

Larry replies, "I thought that was automatic after the judge rendered his/her order. The good thing is I haven't been arrested since then."

Larry was very embarrassed about his arrest record being put out on the air.

Meathead said, "You must've been desperate to have to pay for some pussy."

"Does Vivien know about this?" asked Destiny.

"No, she doesn't. All this happened before I met her." Larry replied.

Marley chimes in, "How many did you get, and how much did you pay?"

Larry was getting pissed with Marley's sarcasm.

"I did it quite a few times and I'd usually pay $10 for a quick blowjob."

Grover empathetically asked, "How did the arrest go down?"

Larry explains how the arrest went down.

"I was driving through the neighborhood and I saw this hot chick walking as I drive past her. We both make eye contact. I pull up to her and she'll say something like, 'Hey baby, you looking for a good time?' I would say yes I am. I ask her what kind of good time are we talking about? She would say, 'I do stuff from just a quickie to full on fucking.' I said that I only have time for a quick blowjob. She said, 'Okay, how much you got?' I said $10, and at that moment, the police jumped out, dragged me out of my car, arrested me, and put me into the back seat of the police car. I never felt so embarrassed in my life."

Destiny asked, "How did these encounters usually go?"

"I'd drive around checking out different girls, looking for the perfect ten. If I see what I like, I pull up beside her. She would get into my car. I tell her what I want and she'd tell me the price. I pay her first, and then she goes to town."

Meathead chimes in, "Any nudity?"

31

"Of course, the chick gets butt naked showing her full rack. I would feel on them, playing with her nipples. I would reach for her pussy at the same time she was grabbing my long rod. We both jack each other off, then she starts sucking my dick and I'm licking her pussy. Once we're done, we put our clothes back on. She then gets out and goes on to next customer."

Larry continued, "If Vivien was listening to the show right now, she would be furious."

Lucky for Larry, Vivien wasn't listening to the show. They both work during the day. Her workplace has the show's website blocked so she and her co-workers aren't able to listen.

CHAPTER 6

As time went on, Larry worked on the show, meeting some of the biggest names in entertainment. He was able to have his pictures taken with them and even made a photo album.

Vivien was proud of Larry for pursuing his career in radio. But, with him out doing station events, it made Vivien feel like she was being left out. Larry, being a gentleman, has always invited her to these events. This allows her to write articles on what's going on around town.

When Larry was not working at the radio station, he was at his auto parts warehouse job, but still having weekends off.

Vivien, on a whim, called one of the guys she worked with and arranged to have lunch. His name was Ted, and they both knew each other from the town's club heyday. Both used to report on the club scene during that time.

She started to explain that with Larry in radio and working his warehouse job, "We're starting to drift apart, you know what I mean? I went to one these station events with Larry, and listeners crowded around him. Women were excited about meeting him. What about you?"

He answered, "I'm the youngest widower."

Vivien gasped, "What the fuck happened?!"

He somberly responded, "She was killed by a drunk driver about a month ago, life has been rough."

As they ate, Vivien's mind began to wander.

She was thinking, Is there someone out there and I don't know it?

Both gazed into each other's eyes. For that very moment, Vivien forgot she even had a boyfriend.

While Larry was at work, Vivien cooked up a false story so Larry wouldn't suspect what she was doing.

She calls Larry and leaves a voicemail, "Larry, I won't be home. I have to work late. A last minute assignment came up."

Larry listens to the message Vivien left and thought to himself, It happens in her line of work.

All the while Larry was listening to Vivien's voicemail, she was having sex with Ted, her old co-worker.

Later that night, Larry got home from work. Vivien hadn't come from work yet. Larry sat down at the computer to gather material for the next day's show, but noticed something was out of place. Normally, all Internet tabs are closed out, computer off-line, and locked.

The computer was open and online. Thinking something wasn't right, Larry checked the browser's history and confirmed his worst fear. Vivien contacted one of her old co-workers on Facebook.

At that very moment, Vivien walked in, thinking Larry was still at work. She was shocked.

"Larry, what the fuck are you doing spying on me? I thought you trusted me!"

Larry jumped up and yelled, "Excuuuuuuuuuuuuuuse me?"

Vivien was stunned that Larry was able to convey all of his emotions and reveal that he knew she was cheating by just saying two words.

Larry continued, "I thought I could trust you. Have you been talking to this guy the whole time we were together?

Vivien shot back, "No, he contacted me and asked if we could talk. You see, his girlfriend was killed in a car crash by a drunk driver a month ago."

Larry, reading Vivien's facial expression, knew she was up to something. Larry, being observant, noticed a used condom in a plastic bag in her purse. She meant to dispose of it after her little secret hook up.

"What's this!?" Larry asked, his voice shaking and trembling.

Vivien stumbled to answer Larry's question, but knew she wasn't able to lie her way out of it.

"Well, I've never lied to you, nor am I going to start. I sent you the fake voicemail so you wouldn't think I was up to something."

Larry then calmed down a little and listened to what Vivien had to say.

She continued, "With you working two jobs, and me working as well, we were starting to drift apart, you know?"

Larry thought for a minute, she was right in that regard.

"Look, we have to work together," said Larry. "I've always been honest with you. I know how you feel. I'm angry that you cheated on me, but the fact you were willing to confess to me about it makes me want to dump you, but I think our relationship is strong enough. Plus, we've been together so long, we just can't just throw it away."

After a long discussion, Larry and Vivien decided to stay home that night. They both turned off their cell phones, watched a movie, then off to bed.

CHAPTER 7

Another three months went by. Larry's position on the show started expanding. He even had his own movie review segment called Fart Face Films. Larry hated the name, but he loved reviewing the movies. Larry was sure that Marley came up with the name, just to screw with him.

One Friday morning, while the show was on-air, everyone on the show was talking about what they were doing for the weekend.

Larry had to excuse himself, "Hey, guys I have run to the men's room. I had a little accident."

Marley asks, "What happened?"

Larry goes, "Let's just say something I ate didn't exactly agree with my stomach."

Marley slyly said, "Hey Larry, looks like you had an accident in your ass."

"Real funny," Larry said sternly.

Marley couldn't help but make butt jokes.

While Larry was in the bathroom cleaning out his pants, he got a call from Vivien. Vivien called and said there was an emergency at home. Larry tried to keep it off the air. She was bitten by a sewer rat.

Meathead went with Larry to his house, which really pisses Larry off because the whole incident was being broadcast. To make matters worse, Marley and Meathead made a bunch of rat jokes. He caught the rat, and took it out to the woods behind the house. Using his dad's shotgun, he blew its asshole out, killed it, and left the carcass to rot.

CHAPTER 8

Destiny spoke in somewhat of a somber voice, "I have some bad news."

"What?" Grover asked Destiny.

"Everyone knows that my family came from Russia before the fall of Communism. My great-aunt couldn't make the trip. She ran into problems with her passport and the KGB wouldn't let her come over. Well, she passed away from breast cancer. I have to travel to Russia for the funeral. I'll be gone for about a month.

Grover chimes in, "Well, who's going to do your work while you're gone?"

Not a moment goes by when a person walks into the phone screening room. His name is Bob. He is about 5'0", 145 pounds, and had a receding hairline. He had some muscle tone, but not the muscle mass Meathead had. He walks like he's just come out of a gay orgy.

Grover, with a perplexed look on his face, turns to Bob and says, "Bob, tell us a little about your radio background."

Bob stepped up to a microphone and spoke, "To start with, I've only been doing radio for four years, working at a small radio station in Philadelphia. First, I was a night DJ and then moved to producer after the last guy was fired."

Marley asks, "Why, what happened?"

Bob then continued, "He was caught banging a chick in the broom closet on his lunch break."

Grover couldn't believe what he heard.

When Bob saw Larry, he asked Marley, "Who's that?"

Marley explains, "That's Larry, our new guy."

"Really?" said Bob.

During a commercial break in the show, Marley explained to Bob about the prank interview he pulled on Larry three months earlier, when Larry was first hired at the station.

Bob laughed out loud, "I pulled pranks on new hires all the time. Maybe we can get together and pull one on this poor sap."

Marley then told Bob, "I think this guy Larry is out to take my job or get his own air shift. I'm not going to be upstaged by some guy with only marginal radio talent."

What Larry didn't know was that Bob had a reputation for pulling humiliating pranks. In Bob's previous radio job, he pulled one that almost drove an intern to suicide. The intern was doing a podcast, Bob pranked him by calling in as a suicidal person. The intern tried to talk him out of it. As he was talking, Bob played gunshot sound effects to give the impression that the person shot himself. It really was Bob playing this person. When the intern found out he was pranked, he almost killed himself.

Marley said, "Even though Larry has natural talent, unlike me, you have to earn your stripes Bob."

"I know what you mean now, Marley," said Bob.

During the show, Bob and Marley were able to instant message each other without Larry knowing what they were up to.

Marley came up with an idea and messaged it to Bob, Okay here's the plan, we have to trick Larry into dropping an f-bomb. Our station is in serious trouble with the FCC over inappropriate material and Grover is being careful not piss off our big, pussified program director.

Bob messaged back, Say we are going to play a game called, Say the Last Word. Larry knows movie lines pretty good.

That same message was passed to Grover.

The show was on its last hour and Grover spoke, "Okay, we're gonna play a little game called The Last Word. Larry, you should be good at this, you know movie lines pretty well."

Bob and Marley winked at each other out of Larry's eyesight. Meathead randomly picked the movie. Larry had to guess the final word of a line from that movie. Marley then chose a line from the movie, Harlem Nights.

"Okay Larry, ready?" asked Marley in a snickering tone.

"Ready," said Larry.

Marley then read the line, "If you going to take up for quick and them, we can……"

Larry, in his excitement, and without thinking, blurted out, "We can all be some fighting motherfuckers this evening."

At that moment, Grover hit the dump button just in the nick of time to prevent what Larry said from going on the air.

"You can't say that Larry," Grover said, trying to keep his cool.

Afterwards, when the show went off-air, Destiny told Larry, "The program director wants you in his office now."

Ray Hawk was a musician before he took the job as the station's program director.

When Larry came into his office with Grover, he was pissed off to the point that steam was pouring out of his ears. His voice boomed so loud it could shatter his office window.

"What the fuck were you thinking? Who the hell do you think you are? Right now we are in deep shit with the FCC over people swearing on the air. I could fire your little punk ass for that!"

Larry felt terrible about it and vowed it wouldn't happen again. Then, Ray calmed down.

"Okay Larry, I'm sorry that I yelled at you the way I did, only because you are new. We had an incident a while before you were hired. Ky-Mani Jones, a reggae singer, came in for an interview and it got out of hand. The FCC put us on notice. When you step up to that microphone you have to think before you open your mouth."

All the while Larry and Grover were in Ray's office, Bob and Marley were laughing with an evil glee because their little prank worked as planned.

"Can you believe how pissed off Ray was at Larry?" Marley asked Bob.

"Yeah, he was so pissed off. I love it. That should knock him down a few pegs," Bob replied.

Marley continued, "I also heard that if Larry swears one more time he'll be canned. The station is still in hot water from the last F-bomb that was dropped when that reggae singer, Ky-Mani Jones, was in the studio. Grover asked him a question about his parents and how they met. It really rubbed him the wrong way. The interview went south real quick."

Then Grover sat Larry down and explained to him what happened and why he needs to be careful about what he says on-air.

CHAPTER 9

As time went on, Marley and Bob became the show's unofficial butt-buddies by hanging out together, and smoking during commercial breaks on the show. On one smoke break, they talked about the next prank to play on Larry.

Some time went by and the show was gearing up for its big festival called Groverfest, the station's biggest event. It gave Marley and Bob another chance to play a more subtle prank on Larry. They all knew that Larry loved music. They went to Grover and proposed their idea.

Marley said to Grover, "Let's have Larry sing, but with a potted down microphone to see if he picks up on it. Then, Bob would roll out on stage inside a plaster replica of Larry and take over singing, ruining his moment to shine."

"Okay," replied Grover.

Earlier on the show, Grover talked about the TV show, Glee, where the cast sang popular songs.

Grover was talking about their terrible remake of Journey's hit song Don't Stop Believing and said, "That was the worst singing I've ever heard. I'll bet our new guy, Larry, could sing that. What do think, Larry?" asked Grover.

Larry spoke and said, "I could sing that but I would need to practice, so I wouldn't mess it up."

Sherlock, the phone screener, chimed in and reminded Larry, "You'll be in front of about 20,000 people, so you can't afford to screw up."

He came up with an ingenious idea to help Larry sing the song correctly. After the show, Sherlock pulled Larry to the side and told him his idea.

"Okay, here's the plan Larry, I'm going to place a laptop on stage. It'll be hidden so only you can see it, showing a karaoke version, so you can keep your vocals in time to the music."

The day of Groverfest came, several bands played, and there was a swimsuit competition.

The time came for Larry to go on stage to sing. The laptop was set up out of view of the audience just like Sherlock told Larry.

Bob had the title changed from, Don't Stop Believing to Don't Stop Sharting.

The lyrics were also changed to match the title of the song. 'Just a small brown turd, his smell makes me want to hurl. Larry has stains in his underwear. Just a shitty boy, busted buying whores on Detroit. He has poop in his pubic hair.'

Larry's face was turning beet-red with anger.

The song continued, 'He has to pay for poon, the smell of grime and fecal fumes. His diaper is as dark as night, the stains go on and on.'

Larry was clenching his fists trying to keep his composure.

Then, the song went into the chorus, 'Don't stop sharting,' as the microphone was potted up, but the second Larry began to sing, the sound engineer got the signal to pot down the mic. Then, a plaster version of Larry rolled onto the stage. It was outfitted with speakers and Bob was inside doing the vocals using a headset microphone. As Bob was singing the altered version of the song, Larry grew angrier and angrier with each line being sung. Marley was laughing. After Larry had finished the audience was also laughing. Larry was so upset that he kicked the plaster replica then rolled it off the edge of the stage. It crashed to the ground and broke into pieces and bruised Bob.

He then went backstage to the trailer and slammed a few beers. In a very disgusted mood, he thought to himself, Somebody is fucking with me, but who? I can't accuse someone without proof; it would make me look like an asshole.

Marley came to console him, even though they knew what they did.

Marley said, "Hey Larry, what happened? Everything was good to go."

Larry said, "Something happened to the microphone causing it to lose power, and this plaster replica of me comes out and cock-blocks me saying all this bullshit about me then finishes the song. I say some jackass just wants to fuck with me."

Marley changed the subject quickly to throw Larry off, believing Larry may have figured out Marley and Bob's prank.

CHAPTER 10

A couple of weeks went by and the holiday season was coming up. This was a special time. It's Larry and Vivien's favorite time of year to reflect on the year's events. They also know, despite what Vivien did, Larry tried to forgive her and talked at length about it. They made adjustments to balance work and time with each other.

On Christmas day, both exchanged gifts with friends and family. Vivien got Larry a Fossil aviator's watch. Larry's gift to Vivien was a handmade necklace from Ireland. Larry had to go behind Vivien's back to arrange for it to be made by her grandparents, who were still living in Ireland. Then he had it shipped to the house in time to surprise her. When she opened it, her eyes lit up so bright you could've been blinded.

She also prepared a large turkey dinner for family and friends. After dinner, Larry and Vivien would put the leftovers in plastic containers. The roasting pan she cooked the turkey in came with a clear plastic cover to keep it moist.

The show was on break from Christmas until after New Year's Day. That gave Marley and Bob time to plan their next prank to play on Larry.

Bob called Marley, "I have a great idea. Let's prank both Larry and his hot, Irish girlfriend."

"What's the plan?" asked Marley.

Bob goes, "Let's trick them into going into a gay nightclub. That would be good for some laughs, right?"

"Right," said Marley.

Bob continues, "Larry said he wouldn't go into a gay nightclub. I'm going to prove him wrong."

Larry and Vivien had a romantic dinner at their favorite diner, Lenny and Denny's, which was owned by twins. Larry and Vivien were regulars. Then, they decided to go out dancing and watch the ball drop on TV at the club, to ring in the New Year.

Larry's phone rang; it was Marley on the other end.

"Hey Larry, there's this new nightclub that just opened up, called The Brown Eye. Why don't you and Vivien check it out?"

Upon entering the club, Larry was shocked at what he saw; two guys hugging, tongue kissing, and grabbing each other's asses.

"Let's get the flying fuck out of here and go home. I can't believe it's a gay bar. I didn't even know."

Vivien drew from her knowledge of the bar scene, and tried to tell Larry that gay bars and nightclubs don't advertise. She felt bad about it, and Larry let it roll off his back. Just like guys in the club let spooge roll off their back.

When the show came back from the holiday break, Grover and everyone else on the show was talking about what they did over the holidays.

Marley spoke, "So, Larry, what did you do over the break?"

Larry replied, "Me and Vivien spent time with her parents, exchanged gifts, and went out on New Year's Eve."

Bob ran in the phone screening room and chimed in, "Hey Larry, what club did you and Vivien go to?"

Larry responded, "A place called The Brown Eye, why?"

At that moment, Marley revealed the joke he and Bob pulled on Larry and Vivien.

"That's a gay club, didn't you know that?!"

Larry, trying very hard to keep his composure because he knew what would happen if he didn't, yelled, "You piece of trashed DNA, you tricked me and Vivien into going to a gay club!"

"Yeah, we did trick you into going to a gay club, but not putting your arm around a guy dressed like Cher," teased Bob.

That really set Larry off because he'd never go into a gay night-club. Larry was yelling into the microphone and near over-modulating the speakers. As angry as Larry was, Marley and Bob were getting a kick out of seeing Larry almost lose his temper, but Larry didn't give them the satisfaction. They believe Larry was hiding something, but didn't know what it was.

Now, Grover knew at this point the pranks were getting out of control. He pulled Bob and Marley off to the side after that day's show.

"Look you guys, I like Larry, and he has a lot of potential to succeed in radio. Both of you need to stop dicking with him so much," Rover said. "I'll tell you why. Something like this happened at my old radio job in Seattle. A guy was pulling pranks on an intern and they got out of hand, guess what happened?"

"Well, what happened?" asked Marley.

Grover answered Marley's question.

"That intern is now in prison for felonious assault. He beat this guy to an inch of his life. It took five people to break it up. He would've killed the person pulling the jokes. He suffered lots of cuts, bruises, 3 broken ribs, a dislocated jaw, a broken nose, a fat lip, one eye shut, and a fractured skull from having punches rained down on him. He spent 5 days in the hospital."

Bob and Marley took what Grover said seriously and decided to lay off Larry for a while. During that time, Larry was thinking to himself, Whoever is fucking with me must not want me to succeed in radio, but why, and what did I do?"

He went home and spoke to Vivien about what he thinks.

Vivien says, "Listen, there's always going to be someone out there that's trying to derail your career, even the very people you work with. I think there are two you should keep an eye on."

"Okay, I'll do that. But if I find out it's them, there's going to be hell to pay and blood on the microphone."

Marley and Bob found a more subtle way to dick with Larry.

Bob went to Sherlock, the phone screener, "Sherlock, what do you think of Larry?"

Sherlock said, "I like Larry. He's a good guy; comes to all his appearances on time and works hard to help the show."

Bob then follows up, "We need you to help us dick with Larry in a more subtle manner using the callers this time."

Sherlock caves in, "What do want me to do?"

Marley then tells Sherlock his idea.

"Whenever Larry gets on the mic and callers call in, tell them to make a negative comment about Larry and his girlfriend to get him riled up so that he would swear."

"Why do you want to do that, Marley?" asked Sherlock.

"Because I can't stand the fact that he's got talent and could replace me, or any one of us on the show," said Marley. "The other reason is that I'm under scrutiny from management because I got into a bar fight just before Larry was hired. I want to take the focus off me, and put it on Larry. I'd rather see him get fired than me."

The week was drawing to a close. Larry was looking forward to spending the weekend with Vivien and to try to mend his relationship with her, despite the fact she cheated and hurt him. She cheated, but Larry did motorboat a chick. He thought one dick was worth a hundred motorboats. But she was the only girl Larry ever dated, and he was the only guy she really ever liked. Both agreed that they had too much time invested in their relationship to just let it fall apart.

Mario, his boss at his auto parts job, called.

"Larry, can you come in on Sunday? One of the guys is sick, and I need coverage for at least three hours."

"Okay, no problem," said Larry.

Vivien heard the conversation.

"Larry, you know we have plans this weekend, right?"

"Yes, I do, but Mario just needs me on Sunday. Our plans are on Friday and Saturday. We really don't do anything on Sunday and we could save extra money, so we can visit Ireland to see your grandparents."

Vivien was relieved that Larry didn't have to work Friday and Saturday. They'll be going to a friend's wedding in Charlotte, North Carolina, which is a nine-hour drive. They were leaving that Friday after the show, and will be back late Sunday morning in time for Larry to work at the auto parts warehouse. Larry didn't mind the 9-hour drive; he needed to pick up milk in Cincinnati anyways.

CHAPTER 11

During that weekend, Bob and Marley got together trading ideas on how to make Larry really lose it.

"Doesn't Larry have a vintage 1985 Chevette?" Bob asked.

"That's right," said Marley.

Then Bob came up with an idea.

"Okay Marley, here's the plan. We get some baby food and plant it in his car. Those old cars from the early eighties are easy to break into without anyone knowing about it."

"Sounds good," Marley said.

Bob continues to explain his plan, "I heard he and Vivien are going out of town for a wedding and won't be back until Sunday morning."

"How do we plant the baby food in Larry's car if he's driving it out there?" asked Marley.

"They're driving Vivien's car this time," Bob answered. "He only drives his Chevette to and from work so that he doesn't put too many miles on it. Vivien has a 2010 Honda CRV."

"Perfect!" exclaimed Marley.

That next day Bob and Marley went to Larry's house to put their prank into action. Bob got a slim jim, a favorite tool car thieves use, to jimmy open a car door without leaving any evidence of it happening. Bob slipped the slim jim between the window and door structure.

"Got it," said Bob, as he heard the lock click. "Give me the baby food and I'll put it in the trunk, that's part one. The next part is on Monday's show when we get Grover to ask Larry about his car, then I ask if he ate baby food."

At that same time, Larry and Vivien were enjoying themselves at their friend's wedding. They were preparing to return home and get ready for the week ahead, unaware Bob and Marley put baby food in his car.

That Monday morning Larry was driving to work, unaware the baby food was in his trunk in the spare tire compartment. He opened the trunk to get his laptop and spotted something made of glass. Bob saw it out of the corner of his eye and made note of it to ambush Larry later, on-air.

On the show, one of the topics was about bullying and the different ways each member of the show handled it.

Grover spoke first, "I remember when I was in school, kids picked on me a lot because my mom had this really junky looking car that she brought me to school in, but it ran and the engine purred like a cat. So, I got back at them. My Mom gave it to me as my first car, and then my dad and I took the body apart and completely rebuilt it. My dad's hobby was rebuilding cars. Marley and Sherlock, how about you guys?"

Sherlock, the phone screener, spoke first because he had to screen the callers and had to keep it short.

"Me, I'll admit I was a bully. I liked to pick on smaller kids because they couldn't fight back. My dad found out and whipped my ass. He told me, 'Now you know what it's like to get your ass whipped and I'm smaller than you son.' "

"Wow," said Grover in amazement. "Marley, what about you?"

"Well, I was the kid that prided myself on using brains over brawn. I was challenged to a debate on politics by some kid who thought he knew it all, and I beat him at his own game."

Then Grover turned to Larry, "How about you Larry, were you ever bullied as a kid?"

Larry answered, "Yes, I too was bullied as a kid. There was this one kid who took money from others and then tried it on me; not once, but twice, he succeeded. The third time landed him in the hospital. I beat the dog shit out of him and nearly got expelled from school. My parents were pissed."

Marley asks, "So, what happened?"

Larry continued, "I told the Principal that I warned him the next time you bother me, I'll knock your teeth down your fucking throat you fat piece of shit. Lucky for me, I only got suspended for ten days. I learned from that day on to avoid getting into fights."

Grover asked, "By the way, who owns the vintage car outside?"

Larry spoke up, "I do. It's a 1985 Chevette. My dad and I restored it before he died in late December 2001. I've been driving it just to and from work."

Then Bob came in the studio.

"I have a quick question for Larry. Do you eat baby food by chance?"

Larry gave Bob that knife in the eyes look.

"I haven't eaten baby food since I was one and a half years old, why?"

Bob responds, "Well, I saw you getting your laptop out of your trunk and saw jars of baby food in your trunk."

Larry's temper really flared.

"Okay, you gay wad son of a bitch, let's go to my car and I'll prove there's no baby food in the trunk. C'mon you little pole-smoking, tube-steak-eating, mother fucker!" screamed Larry, as they both went down to Larry's car.

He opened the trunk. Larry was shocked at what he saw. What happens next nearly got Larry fired and arrested. He grabbed Bob and threw him to the ground with a Greco-Roman style take down and started beating on Bob until he was crying like a little baby. Larry hit him with the Stone Cold Stunner, then DDT'd him into the ground while he begged for mercy.

Marley came down and told Larry to stop. Larry did stop and Bob was a bloody and bruised mess. Destiny and Grover were both upset by what happened.

"What the fuck are you doing Larry? Have you lost your fucking mind?! You're probably going to get fired!" Grover's voice was rising with every word.

At that moment, Ray Hawk, hearing the commotion came outside and shouted, "Larry I want your dumbass in my office now!" he said in booming voice. "And the rest of you, too."

Grover and the others had one collective thought, Oh, shit!

All sat in Ray's office, "Just tell me what the fuck happened out there."

Larry spoke first, knowing he could be fired, arrested, or both.

"I won't mince words. I fought with Bob because I think that he planted baby food in my trunk to dick with me."

"Well, I will not tolerate fighting," Ray said harshly. "Thank your lucky stars that someone didn't call the police!"

Everyone left Ray's office, except for Larry and Bob.

"Okay, you two assholes, I want to know what's up, now!"

Bob and Larry were shaking nervously for two very different reasons. Larry might lose his job. If Bob fesses up, he'll wind up as another bloody mess.

Bob spoke first, just so he could leave. "Ray, I planted the baby food in Larry's car while he was out of town for the weekend because I thought it would be a good prank."

Larry, in a real ominous tone said, "Do not fuck with me again you little midget, or you'll find yourself eating your own teeth mixed with that baby food! You understand?! When I was a little kid growing up, I didn't fit in with the popular crowd. One time, a kid bullied me one too many times."

"What ha-ha-happened?" asked Bob in a shaky voice.

Larry answered, "I beat the living shit out of him, and then I got suspended from school for ten days. That's what happened. I'm a pretty level-headed person. Don't piss me off, which is what you and that kid did."

Ray then screamed, "Enough! Larry...Bob...I'm suspending both of you knuckleheads for ten days."

Larry came home from work that afternoon. Vivien was making BLT sandwiches for lunch.

She turned around and asked, "Larry, baby, how was your day?"

"Miserable. I got suspended for 10 days for fighting and was told if it happens again I'll be fired."

Vivien's face turned into a combination of anger and concern. She was angry because Larry broke the number one workplace rule:

don't fight. He was concerned because someone was pulling pranks on Larry for no reason other than to get a rise out of him.

CHAPTER 12

Over the ten days during the suspension period, Larry worked at his warehouse job. Mario, his boss, called him into his office.

"Larry, I'm afraid I have to reduce your hours. Business is slow and we have competition from a bigger rival. Also, a fellow employee snapped a picture of you sleeping. Is that true?"

"No, I closed my eyes for .2 seconds. I had something on my mind," Larry replied.

He was a little upset, but he understood.

"Larry, you are an excellent worker. I've had to do the same with the others."

"I understand," said Larry.

When the suspension was over, Larry was back on the show. They were talking about their next event coming up, a mankini car wash to raise money for the local food bank and help other community organizations.

The next morning everyone dressed in bikinis. Larry put his underwear into his backpack. The mankini car wash was a thrilling success, raising over $1,000,000.00.

Larry went to get his underwear out of his backpack, but they were not there. While he was in the studio, Bob snuck into Larry's backpack and took his underwear.

Larry said, "I couldn't find them."

Marley gave Larry a clean pair from the pack that was bought for a previous segment.

Bob rushes into the studio.

"I think Larry has a dirty little secret. Look at this!"

Bob held up the pair of underwear that Larry was going to change back into.

Grover was shocked, "What is that?!"

Larry tried to explain the faded skid mark.

"I washed that pair about two times using bleach that apparently wasn't strong enough to clean it," Larry said, defending himself.

Over the next week, Bob and Marley made corny jokes about the situation. Those two were real nuts, but not as nutty as Larry's soiled underpants. During the time when Bob hid Larry's underwear, Marley made parody songs about him with titles like, Wham - Wake Me Up Before You Doo Doo, Scat Benatar – Fartbreaker, etc.

That next day, two events happened, pushing Larry past his breaking point. Marley and Bob never returned Larry's underwear.

"We have a surprise for you, Larry" Grover said.

"What's that?" asked Larry in a voice seething with pent up anger. "As if I haven't endured enough juvenile nonsense?"

Marley was trying to contain his laughter.

"Okay, close your eyes Larry," Bob said to him.

Larry sat at his microphone, and at that moment, Marley brought in a small display case containing Larry's underwear with the faded skid mark from Larry's attempts to clean them.

"What the hell is that?!" Larry exclaimed.

Bob, in a snickering manner said, "Our tribute to you."

Larry just exploded, and in one swift punch, he broke the case. Glass shattered everywhere in the studio.

Marley was so mad that Larry broke the case. He said, "What the fuck, Larry? How would you like it if I smashed your laptop?"

Larry decided to beat Marley to the punch. He picked up his own laptop and smashed it to the ground. Marley was so mad that Larry was smart enough to smash his own laptop before anyone could get the chance. Larry really showed Marley who the boss was.

Larry then bandaged his hand and headed home. Vivien was there with her bags packed. Normally she takes short trips out of town to cover concerts.

"Are you going to cover another concert in the next town?" Larry asked.

He knew and accepted that was part of her job.

"No, I'm leaving for Los Angeles, and I'm leaving you."

"Why?" asked Larry. "You constantly keep dodging the subject of us."

Vivien replied, "What subject was that?"

"I mean I did everything the best I could to balance work, and being with you. All of our audience believes I've been good to you," Larry said, trying to figure out Vivien's rationale.

"Look, I know I've always loved and respected you. I'm sorry for what happened between me and Ted, I still regret that. It's about us getting married maybe. I can't wait any longer. Four years is long enough. I'm sorry Larry. If you can't commit yourself to me, I can no longer be with be with you, so goodbye."

But, before Vivien left she said, "Larry, I want one more thing."

"What's that?" Larry asked.

Vivien gave Larry that seductive look in her eyes and said, "I want you to fuck my brains out so I have something to remember you by. You always gave me the best sex I've ever had, and I need just one more taste of that huge long rod of yours!"

Larry carried her one last time up the stairs. They slowly took each other's clothes off. He started to feel on her soft, smooth skin, just as he did before. He played with her nipples until they were rock hard. She began massaging his rod and started sucking on it. In what seemed like an eternity, he began licking and sucking on her smooth, polished pussy both moaning and groaning. This time, she got on top, using the same pumping action a guy uses on a girl, up and down, up and down.

After five minutes, both squirted at the same time and screamed loudly, "OH MY GOD THAT WAS AWESOME!!"

The next morning, while Larry was sleeping, Vivien got up and fetched her bags and left. For the first time in four years, Larry was alone. His life is now a shattered mess.

He went to the cemetery to place flowers on his parent's grave. While there, he saw a gravesite with his name on it. It was his parent's intent to have the whole family buried together. Larry was very close to his parents being that he was an only child.

CHAPTER 13

He thought everyone on the show dicked with him in one way or another. Who did it the worst and why? He knew Meathead, Destiny, and Grover busted his balls often, but in a manner that wasn't rude. Sherlock, the phone screener, would tell the callers what to say to get Larry riled up. Larry found that out when a friend of his, interning in the promotions department at the station, told him. As for Bob and Marley, even Vivien, his now ex-girlfriend, advised him to watch those two. Another person also had inside information about the pranks Bob and Marley played on Larry. It was the I.T. guy, Jeff Hardwig.

He and Larry sat down to lunch one afternoon, and he told Larry everything he knew.

"Okay, Larry, I'm telling you this because you have potential, but your temper is going to get you fired. It is also the reason why they mess with you. They want to get a rise out of you, and because Marley is insanely jealous of your talent, since he has none," he said.

Larry took the information, digested it, and thought, Now there's going to be bloody hell to pay, and I'll die if I have to. Remembering all the times he's been pranked on and humiliated, his only thought was that there would be blood on the microphone before this day is out.

Larry went home and he found some military surplus that his uncle bought for him. It consisted of an armored vest, a .45 caliber pistol, and an Uzi compact machine gun with two empty clips, one for each gun. Larry went on an occasional hunting trip with his uncle, a retired Marine.

Then he went to a military surplus store and bought a black pair of army boots, a S.W.A.T. uniform, and a box of hollow point bullets.

"Perfect," Larry said to himself.

He knew they exploded upon exiting the body.

"Uh, can I help you find anything?" the store owner asked.

"No," Larry replied, "Just getting some stuff for a hunting trip."

"Oh, okay," said the store owner.

Larry returned home later that day. He started going over his plan, keeping in mind he'll either die or go to prison. If he had to die, it would be on his own terms. One idea was to just shoot everyone and then himself in the middle of the show. Another was to shoot them, but not kill them. He mulled over it through the night, and by dawn a decision was made.

CHAPTER 14

To buy himself some time, he called Bob on his cell phone.

"Bob, listen, I'm running a little late this morning. I had to jump start Vivien's car."

The show was still unaware that Vivien had broken up with Larry.

Larry arrived at the radio station dressed like he was about to enter a war zone. Nobody knew he had a gun on him or what he had in mind. Everyone thought it was related to a show segment.

Meanwhile, in the studio, Grover was ranting on-air. "Destiny, do you have to polish your nasty toenails during the show?" Grover asked, sarcastically.

"Geez, come on! Your nail polish smells like Larry's stained underwear," said Marley as he was handing Grover an e-mail about Larry, from a listener who'd heard the argument between Larry and Vivien two days ago.

At that moment, Larry walks into the studio.

Bob goes, "What's with the G.I. Joe getup you got on, Larry Jafart?"

"What do you think, you little ass licking, pole-smoking faggot?" Larry asked in a very sinister tone.

"Looks like you're a soldier," Marley said teasingly.

Not even a second goes by, Larry pulls out both guns and starts shooting, spraying the whole studio with a rain of gunfire. He was shooting until the first gun was emptied. Then, using the Uzi, continued shooting until its clip was emptied. Bob was killed instantly by the first burst of gunfire, but the others were severely injured and barely survived.

By the time the paramedic squads responded, shell casings were scattered all over the place, and blood was splattered everywhere. Larry escaped the building, down a rarely used back stairwell. He got in his car, heading towards his planned suicide point, the Pearl River Bridge. But Larry had other plans to deal with everyone on the show who pushed him to his breaking point.

Meanwhile, back at the radio station, there was blood everywhere, even dripping from the mics, control board, computers, and other equipment. Grover, Destiny, and Meathead tried to duck for cover, but were hit also. They started to administer first aid on each other, until the paramedics arrived. Marley was lucky enough to slip out into the studio hallway, as Larry sprayed the studio with gunfire. A few bullets hit the breaker box behind Grover's chair. Sparks were flying all over and Grover's hat had metal in it. The metal conducted electricity, shocking him to death. Destiny and Meathead were very badly wounded in Larry's second hail of gunfire. The paramedics were able to get them stabilized and to the hospital quickly.

Marley, thinking he had outwitted Larry, was running through an alley, between buildings, looking for a hiding place. Larry was just around the next corner and grabbed him in a chokehold and yanked him back behind a dumpster. He pulled on his hair and started beating the daylights out of him. Marley was bloodied and bruised, begging for mercy.

"Why should I show you mercy?" Larry asked in a very sinister voice. "You and that pole-smoking faggot Bob did everything possible to derail my radio career."

"Come on, I was just busting your balls," Marley pleaded.

"And now I'm busting yours," Larry said as he crushed Marley's testicles under his army boot. Larry took out a 6" hunting knife and slit Marley's throat, ear to ear. Blood just gushed out like crimson red lava from a volcano.

Sherlock wasn't in the studio during Larry's massacre because he had to leave to take one of his legendary dumps in the restroom down the hall. The restroom near the studio was out of order, and Larry didn't know where he was. When Sherlock got back to the studio and saw the blood splattered carnage Larry had left behind, he slipped and fell in the pool of blood. He cracked his skull open and his blood was mixed with Bob's AIDS tainted blood and died at the hospital two days later, from infection and loss of blood. Nobody knew that Bob contracted HIV from having anal and oral sex with men.

In the meantime every news outlet in town and across the country reported on what happened. Larry was now being hunted by the police for days after the initial shootings.

Larry then found out which gym Meathead works out at. Larry had an idea. He rigged up a weight machine with explosives to be triggered by weight. Knowing Meathead's training regimen, he rigged the bomb to go off at 245 pounds. When he picked up the barbell at the set weight, it would detonate.

Meathead got to the gym, and set the machine at 245 pounds. On his first lift, the bomb detonated and shards of metal, blood, and guts went flying everywhere. It even blew out the front window of the gym.

Destiny, not knowing what happened to the others, was driven home from the hospital by a friend of hers from her news anchor days. What she didn't know was that while she was at the hospital, Larry snuck into her house and doused her tampons with cyanide poison.

Destiny went to use the bathroom, grabbed a poisoned tampon just as Larry had planned, and stuck it into her pussy.

When she turned on the TV there was wall-to-wall coverage on every news outlet in the country. She was so shocked at all the bloody carnage Larry had left behind. She started to shake so bad that her heartbeat skyrocketed, causing a blood vessel to burst and mix with the cyanide. She died within an hour after the tampon was used.

Larry was looking in the window of Destiny's house and saw her slump forward at her computer desk. He slipped into the darkness of the night, even though every cop in Pearl City was looking for him.

Police departments in the surrounding communities set up road-blocks to stop him from escaping. He knew the police would look for him at his house. When they got there they found a hand-drawn floor plan of the radio station building, the surrounding area, and a list of items Larry needed in order to carry out his plan. Unknown to the police, Larry was hiding out in his uncle's hunting cabin, deep in the woods, overlooking the city. His uncle is a retired U.S. Marine and taught him how to hunt, fish, and live off the land.

At sunrise, Larry made his way to the bridge just as he planned. The moment he got out of his car, the police surrounded him quickly, with guns drawn. He stepped onto the railing and paused.

With a megaphone, an officer started to convince Larry to step down and surrender. As a precaution the entire bridge was closed to traffic in both directions. Traffic had to be rerouted around it.

Thoughts went racing through his mind of what led to this. All I wanted was a career in broadcasting. Two of my co-workers didn't like me. Vivien dumps me because I wasn't prepared for marriage. I dropped an f-bomb on-air, beat the shit out that faggoty, pole-smoker Bob, and nearly got fired. Then I just killed six people in the span of a week.

The bridge was completely closed to traffic. Larry was completely surrounded by police and had nowhere to run.

"Please step down from the rail. Put your hands on the back of your head," the officer commanded.

Larry was zoned out, not even hearing the police. Larry then took a look to the sky; it was a gloomy, hazy day. He could see a storm coming in from the distance. This is not what Larry wanted to do today. Larry thought to himself, Man this is perfect cranking weather.

The police screamed, "Get the FUCK DOWN," instantly snapping him out of his daydream.

Larry, as if he was about to comply, then turned to face the police with guns drawn. He held up his fist then flipped the middle finger.

Larry said just three words, "BOBBLE MY DONG!" then jumped off the bridge, falling one hundred and fifty feet to his death in the valley below.

His body splattered all over a moving car below, causing an epic pile up on the road. The driver of that car was Vivien, Larry's now ex-girlfriend, who was on her way to Los Angeles. She was instantly killed by the impact of Larry's body landing on the car's windshield and roof, causing both to collapse.

What Larry was hiding from the show was that he knew Vivian was bi-sexual. She left him for a woman living in L.A.

Police and paramedics all responded to the scene, and pulled their bloodied, lifeless bodies from the wreck. For some strange, mysterious reason Larry, even though he was dead, had this grin on his face. He was finally going home.

CHAPTER 15

His uncle came to the Pearl City morgue to claim Larry's body and prepare it for burial. He found the suicide note Larry wrote the night before, even containing his burial wishes. It read: "All I wanted in life is to be successful. I tried very hard. Certain people treated me like I was some doormat or were just jealous of me. I made my own mistakes in life that I regretted. Losing mom & dad while they were enjoying life to the fullest, and looking forward to me and Vivian's relationship blossoming into something more. Whatever happens to me as a result of the events today, I wish to fulfill my parents' final request in their will that I'm to be buried with them."

There was a second item found in the mangled wreckage. It was a manuscript of a short novel about a fictional person getting into radio. This person gets picked on endlessly and loses it. It tells the details of how he murders everyone. Anyone reading the book would've known to stop fucking with Larry before it was too late. It's too bad the police found the manuscript after Larry committed suicide.

If only someone had a clue of the book's existence before he killed everyone. If only someone was lucky enough to read the book before the rampage, all of this would've been prevented. It would've served as a warning to everyone.

That's not how life works. It's too bad that life isn't like the movies or novels, and no one ever holds in their hands a perfect plan of how a murdering psycho would kill everyone before he did it. It's just too bad. And to think that Larry Jarocque was writing a book about a fictional character named Jeffrey LaRocque.

At the funeral home Larry's casket was closed. His body was so mangled that you couldn't recognize it or even want to look at it.

At the cemetery, under a grey sky, light rain, and a slight rumble of thunder, Larry's friends and family gathered at the gravesite.

The minister spoke, "Larry Jarocque, son and friend to us all, is now finally committed to this grave. Ashes to ashes, and dust to dust," he proclaimed as he picked up a handful of dirt. He then poured it on the casket before it was lowered.

Finally, and for all eternity, Larry Jarocque was not still standing. The entire universe let out a collective "Soooooooooooooooo."